ANIMALS OF THE MOUNTAINS

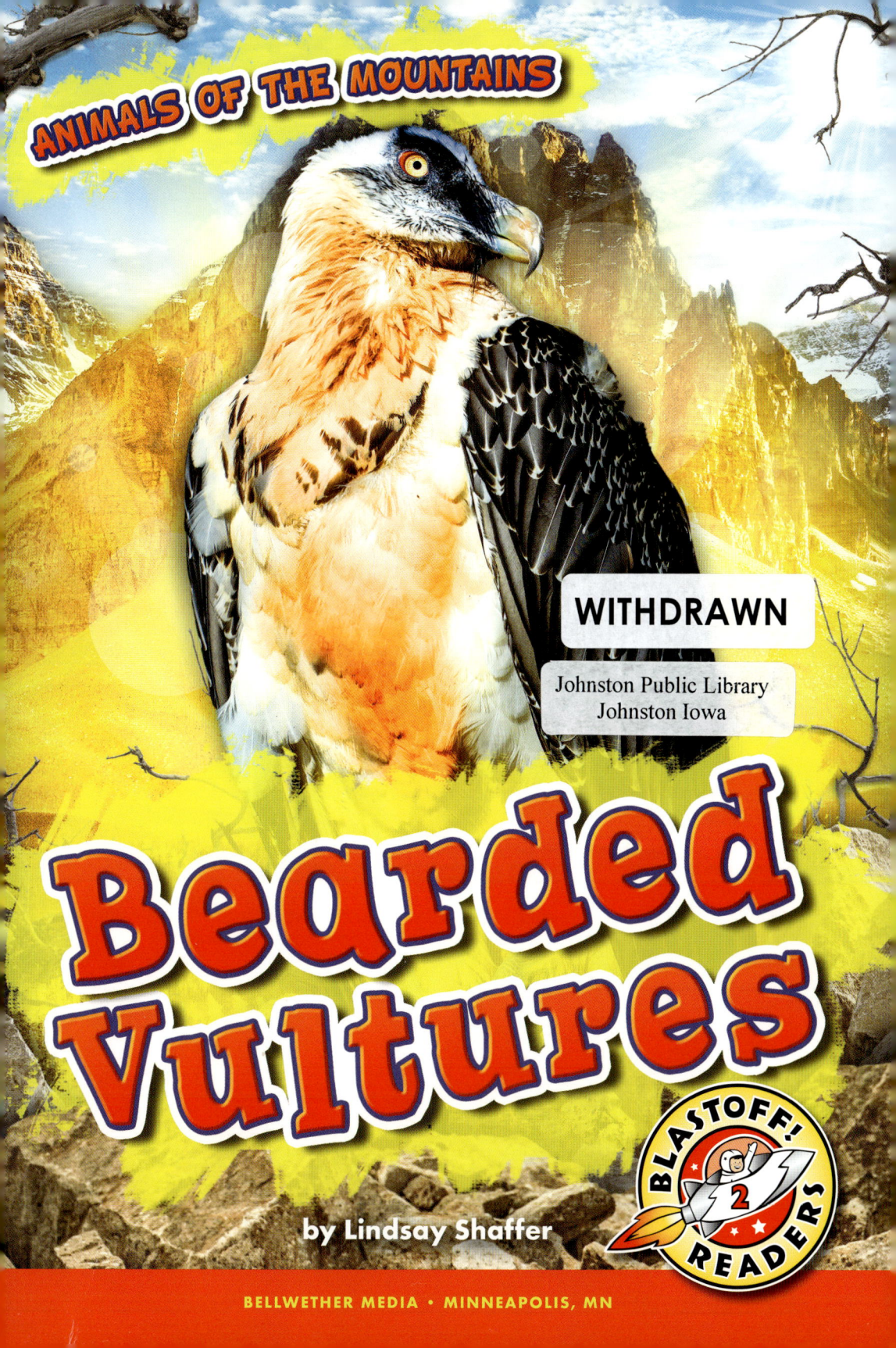

Bearded Vultures

by Lindsay Shaffer

BLASTOFF! READERS 2

BELLWETHER MEDIA • MINNEAPOLIS, MN

Note to Librarians, Teachers, and Parents:

Blastoff! Readers are carefully developed by literacy experts and combine standards-based content with developmentally appropriate text.

Level 1 provides the most support through repetition of high-frequency words, light text, predictable sentence patterns, and strong visual support.

Level 2 offers early readers a bit more challenge through varied simple sentences, increased text load, and less repetition of high-frequency words.

Level 3 advances early-fluent readers toward fluency through increased text and concept load, less reliance on visuals, longer sentences, and more literary language.

Level 4 builds reading stamina by providing more text per page, increased use of punctuation, greater variation in sentence patterns, and increasingly challenging vocabulary.

Level 5 encourages children to move from "learning to read" to "reading to learn" by providing even more text, varied writing styles, and less familiar topics.

Whichever book is right for your reader, Blastoff! Readers are the perfect books to build confidence and encourage a love of reading that will last a lifetime!

This edition first published in 2020 by Bellwether Media, Inc.

No part of this publication may be reproduced in whole or in part without written permission of the publisher. For information regarding permission, write to Bellwether Media, Inc., Attention: Permissions Department, 6012 Blue Circle Drive, Minnetonka, MN 55343.

Library of Congress Cataloging-in-Publication Data

Names: Shaffer, Lindsay, author.
Title: Bearded Vultures / by Lindsay Shaffer.
Description: Minneapolis, MN : Bellwether Media, Inc., [2020] |
   Series: Blastoff! Readers: Animals of the Mountains | Includes bibliographical references and index. |
   Audience: Age 5-8. | Audience: K to Grade 3.
Identifiers: LCCN 2018061015 (print) | LCCN 2019001614 (ebook) | ISBN 9781618915535 (ebook) |
   ISBN 9781644870129 (hardcover : alk. paper)
Subjects: LCSH: Lammergeier--Juvenile literature.
Classification: LCC QL696.F32 (ebook) | LCC QL696.F32 S46 2020 (print) | DDC 598.9/2--dc23
LC record available at https://lccn.loc.gov/2018061015

Text copyright © 2020 by Bellwether Media, Inc. BLASTOFF! READERS and associated logos are trademarks and/or registered trademarks of Bellwether Media, Inc. SCHOLASTIC, CHILDREN'S PRESS, and associated logos are trademarks and/or registered trademarks of Scholastic Inc., 557 Broadway, New York, NY 10012.

Editor: Kate Moening   Designer: Jeffrey Kollock

Printed in the United States of America, North Mankato, MN

Table of Contents

Life in the Mountains	4
A Bird's-eye View	10
Bone Eaters	16
Glossary	22
To Learn More	23
Index	24

Life in the Mountains

Bearded vultures live high in the mountains of Europe, Asia, and Africa.

Powerful icy wind blows in this wintry **biome**!

Bearded Vulture Range

N W E S

range = 🟩

Bearded vultures have **adapted** to the cold. Strong outer feathers help block out wind.

dense leg feathers

Soft, **dense** feathers cover their legs.

7

Some bearded vultures have black ear feathers. These take in extra heat.

black ear feathers

Special Adaptations

strong outer feathers

dense leg feathers

sharp eyes

They help bearded vultures survive freezing weather.

9

A Bird's-eye View

Bearded vultures **perch** on rocky cliffs. This gives them a great view.

Their sharp eyes study the ground for food.

11

These birds also travel far to search for food. Some soar over 100 miles (161 kilometers) in one day!

They use **thermals** to soar without getting tired.

Bearded vultures bathe their feathers in iron-rich water. The iron turns their white feathers red.

feathers after iron bath

without iron bath

Vultures may use their colored feathers to show off! The iron may also help them stay healthy.

15

Bone Eaters

Most vultures eat **carrion**. But bearded vultures would rather eat bones!

They are the only animal to eat mostly bones and **marrow**.

Bearded Vulture Diet

whole bones

marrow

carrion

17

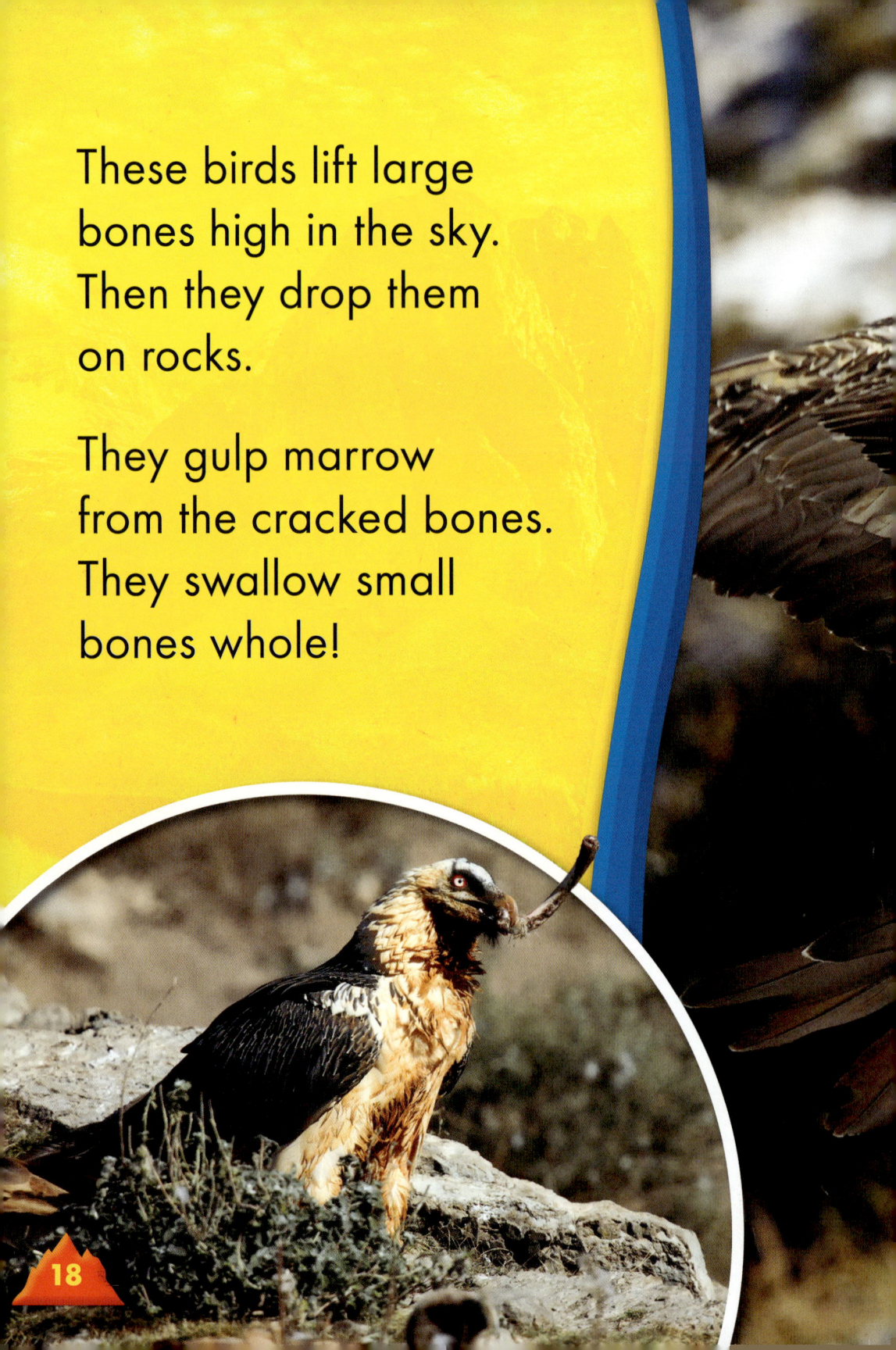

These birds lift large bones high in the sky. Then they drop them on rocks.

They gulp marrow from the cracked bones. They swallow small bones whole!

Bearded Vulture Stats

| Least Concern | Near Threatened | Vulnerable | Endangered | Critically Endangered | Extinct in the Wild | Extinct |

conservation status: near threatened

life span: 22 years

19

Bearded vultures have strong **acid** in their stomachs. The acid quickly breaks down bones.

Inside and out, bearded vultures are built for life in their mountain home!

Glossary

acid—a powerful liquid that breaks down food

adapted—changed over a long period of time

biome—a large area with certain plants, animals, and weather

carrion—the rotting meat of a dead animal

dense—close together

marrow—the soft, inner part of bones

perch—to sit in a high place

thermals—rising currents of warm air

To Learn More

AT THE LIBRARY
Kissock, Heather. *I Am a Vulture*. New York, N.Y.: AV2 by Weigl, 2017.

Sommer, Nathan. *Vultures*. Minneapolis, Minn.: Bellwether Media, 2019.

Waxman, Laura Hamilton. *California Condors: Wide-Winged Soaring Birds*. Minneapolis, Minn.: Lerner Publications, 2016.

ON THE WEB

FACTSURFER

Factsurfer.com gives you a safe, fun way to find more information.

1. Go to www.factsurfer.com.

2. Enter "bearded vultures" into the search box and click 🔍.

3. Select your book cover to see a list of related web sites.

Index

acid, 20
adaptations, 6, 9
Africa, 4
Asia, 4
bathe, 14, 15
biome, 5
bones, 16, 17, 18, 20
carrion, 16, 17
cliffs, 10
colors, 8, 14, 15
Europe, 4
eyes, 9, 10
feathers, 6, 7, 8, 9, 14, 15
food, 10, 12, 16, 17, 18, 20
iron baths, 14, 15
legs, 7, 9
marrow, 17, 18
perch, 10
range, 5
soar, 12, 13

status, 19
stomachs, 20
thermals, 13
weather, 9
wind, 5, 6

The images in this book are reproduced through the courtesy of: Dmitri Gomon, front cover; Karel Bartiki, pp. 4-5, 18, 19; Florent Lacroute, p. 6 (left); imageBROKER/ Alamy, p. 7; Michal Ninger, pp. 8-9; Alta Oosthuizen, p. 9 (vulture), 13; Artem Orlyanskiy, p. 9 (eye); Arco IMages GmbH/ Alamy, p. 10; Gideon Malherbe, pp. 10-11; Emmanuel Rondeau, pp. 12-13; Karel Stepan, p. 14; BorisVetshev, p. 15; Mark Caunt, pp. 14-15; BIOSPHOTO/ Alamy, pp. 16-17; kridsada kamsombat, p. 17 (bones); ivanoel, p. 17 (marrow); Markos Loizou/ Alamy, p. 17 (carrion); David Tipling Photo Library/ Alamy, pp. 20-21; Richard Bartz, p. 21; MarclSchauer, p. 22.